The Wiggle Garden

Kathleen Olson

ISBN   978-1-953821-50-8 Ebook
ISBN   978-1-953821-49-2 Paperback

The EC Publishing LLC books may be ordered
through booksellers or by contacting:

EC Publishing LLC
116 South Magnolia Ave.
Suite 3, Unit F
Ocala, FL 34471, USA
Direct Line: +1 (352) 644-6538
Fax: +1 (800) 483-1813
http://www.ecpublishingllc.com/

Ordering Information:
Quantity sales. Special discounts are available on quantity purchases by corporations, associations, and others. For details, contact the publisher at the address above.

Printed in the United States of America

Table of Contents

Chapter 1

Late in the morning, the king was gently awakened by his servant, Biztha. As Xerxes tried to lift his head off the pillow, his headache prevented the action.

"Would your majesty care for a restorative?" Biztha inquired.

"Now."

Biztha scurried away. What he would bring back would be some very diluted wine with herbs to help him get over his headache quicker, and it included mint leaves to ease his foul breath.

For the past 180 days, King Xerxes had hosted governors, diplomats, satraps, envoys and anyone else who thought of himself a "someone." It was all in honor of his third anniversary on the throne of Persia. Xerxes felt that 180 days was way too long to celebrate such an insignificant milestone. However, given the massive territory of his empire, 127 provinces from India to Cush, also known as the upper Nile, it took some participants easily a month to get to Susa, the capitol. It all depended on their mode of transportation.

He wanted to display the vast wealth of his kingdom along with his own glory. To do that, he had ordered each wine goblet made of gold and each different one from the other. The stewards were instructed to allow each man to drink any amount he pleased. There were hangings of white and blue linen fastened with silver rings on marble pillars. Mosaic pavements had been laid featuring mother-of-pearl, marble of varying shades, and designs of gorgeous purple porphyry and other precious stones.

Each meal was full of the best of the best: sweet sesame cakes, and chickpeas mashed and flavored with olive oil and garlic with plenty of pita bread for dipping. There was rice, crunchy cucumbers, savory kabobs, sweet honey, moist dates, many varieties of olives, and piles of multiple assortments of fruits. And of course there were the king's favorites, delicately munchy baklava, yogurt, schwarma and mulukkeya. Xerxes was particularly fond of schwarma. He loved the rich scent of the 17 different meats piled one on top of the other roasted on a vertical spit and served so it appeared to be in the shape of a desert dust storm.

After the 180 days were over, Xerxes then gave a celebration for those in the Citadel of Susa that lasted seven days, and this would be the seventh day. That evening, when he entered the King's Garden where the banquet was held, all in attendees got on their knees and touched their foreheads to the ground. Xerxes was pleased with these people and took his elevated place at the head table. When he gave his guests permission, they sat down also.

Xerxes had to admit he was really sick and tired of the banquets, but this one seemed entirely lackluster. What a way to end! He wanted to do something spectacular, something that would stand out in everyone's minds that it was something only he could do. That night, he drank the wine. The more he drank the more he wished for something unforgettable to happen. Well, if it were to happen, it was he who would need to make it happen.

Half way through the banquet, an idea came to him. He would call for the Queen to come to his banquet wearing her royal crown. He could show off her beauty to all at the banquet. It would be unforgettable!

He called his servants Mehuman, Biztha, Harbona, Bigtha, Abagtha, Zethar and Carcas over to his table and whispered to them. His message made most of them smile except Mehuman who looked doubtful. But they scurried off into the palace to carry out the directive.

In the meantime, at the other end of the citadel, Queen Vashti was giving a banquet for the women in the royal palace. Her table matched item for item what the men were eating and drinking, although a lot less drinking. After speaking briefly with the queen, Xerxes servants were back soon at the men's banquet. Xerxes looked expectantly to Mehuman, as he was in charge. The servant shook his head no.

Xerxes was outraged. His face turned red and he sputtered at Mehuman, "Tell me what she said!"

"She said, 'No way, no how'!"

His anger burned, and he stormed out of the banquet hall and all in attendance were speechless. And forgotten.

He and his servants ended up in the throne room where he called for men of the law to come to his aid. He paced, and his anger grew greater as he waited for the knowledgeable men to help him understand what could be done to Queen Vashti.

"She said 'no' to me! How dare *she!*" Xerxes mumbled angrily under his breath. "She's not allowed to say 'no.' She's not only my subject, but my wife, and a wife must do as her husband says. *Especially* if she's married to the monarch! She has to set the standard for all wives." And out loud he demanded, "And where are those men?!" They were there within minutes.

When the men arrived, they humbly bowed to the king. The servants brought refreshments and made sure there were comfortable places for the men to sit. When seemingly satisfied with the seating, all three men of the law sat and took out tablets and began to write.

Xerxes, still on edge, bellowed, "Why are you writing anything? I haven't even told you what is going on!"

All three stopped writing and looked at the king expectantly.

"Now, gentlemen, I will tell you what happened," he announced with poorly controlled anger.

One of the men, known as Memucan, said, "I can see that your majesty is very upset. It's our job to help sort things out for you."

The second man, Carshina , added, "Let us take that burden off of you."

Tarshish was the third man. "Please explain to us in detail exactly what happened tonight."

Xerxes did, and the longer he talked, the more he clenched his jaw and the redder his face got.

"Now I see why you were so upset," Tarshish said, nodding.

"No wife has the right to refuse her husband much less the queen to refuse her king," agreed Carshina.

"This will take some work on our part, but I believe we can come to a satisfactory conclusion soon," Memucan stated.

"What do you mean, 'come to a satisfactory conclusion soon'. I want satisfaction *now!*" Xerxes yelled at them. "The conclusion is that my wife defied me." The yelling was turned up a decibel. "Period, end of sentence!" The king then took a deep breath and, in a strained tone of voice, asked what they were going to advise him to do about it. He still shook with anger.

"If I may, Sire," Tarshish asked.

Xerxes nodded.

"You would be perfectly within your rights to have her killed."

"I thought of that."

"Something to inform the public has to be done," said Memucan. "You just can't let her go scot-free. Because when it gets out what happened, and it will since Vashti is the main source of gossip in Susa, I'm afraid wives all over the empire will feel it is all right to defy their husbands."

"That could lead to disharmony, chaos and the ruin of the Persian Empire," Xerxes followed with a touch a fear in his voice. "You are so right! We must not let her off the hook. "But how is the best way to do it?"

"Majesty, may I speak?" asked Carshina.

Xerxes motioned to him.

"My suggestion would be to issue a Royal Decree that Vashti never be permitted in your presence again and would be banished from the kingdom. Of course, the decree would contain why this was being done and that would cool any female rebellion. You are a strong leader and your people will respect your reason."

Somewhat calmer, Xerxes demanded that she be banished that night. It was done.

"Majesty," Memucan inquired hours after Vashti was gone, "I can see that you are still full of anger. I have been thinking about your situation. See if this works for you. Why don't we make a search of your realm for beautiful young maidens. Appoint commissioners in every province to bring these girls to the Citadel of Susa. Give the girls time-honored beauty treatments and then the girl that pleases the king the most will be made queen in place of Vashti."

Memucan's proposal appealed to the king.

Chapter 2

It was later in the morning than Hadassah would have liked, and she regretted the folly of taking time to eat her morning meal. She grabbed her sewing basket and ran out of the yard past the pomegranate trees and her beloved rose garden.

Hadassah arrived at the Kings Gate in Susa to find her friends sitting there already with their workbaskets on their laps. She sat down next to Merab and peered at her work. She enjoyed Merab's company but her work was not the most salable, whereas Hadassah's work, embroidery on delicate fabric, was in demand.

Also at the King's Gate was her cousin, Mordecai who had a position at the King's palace. Hadassah was an orphan and he had adopted her. Mordecai was very kind to her and looked out for her every need, and she loved him dearly. Above all, it was his company and wisdom that she sought.

"Hey, Squirt, why so late?" Naomi asked Hadassah.

Hadassah hated being called "Squirt" even if she was the shortest in the group.

"Sorry. I had a new idea for a pattern and couldn't wait to try it out."

"What of?" Mereb inquired.

"A butterfly, but you know that big orange and black ones?"

"Oh, you mean the one they call the Traveler?"

"Is that what they call it?" Mara came in. "Oh, and by the way, do you know what I heard?" She said changing the subject. Mara was very fond of gossip.

"What?" Everyone chimed in with varying amounts of enthusiasm. For the most part, gossip bored Hadassah, but Mara was going to say whatever she had in mind no matter what.

"I heard what color Queen Vashti is favoring this season."

"I hope it's not yellow," Naomi moaned. "I look a fright in yellow."

"No, it's not yellow, it's pink."

"Almost as bad as yellow," Naomi grumbled.

"There's nothing that says you have to wear pink," Hadassah directed. "Come on girls, let's concentrate a little bit on our work."

And the work went on, but not without the usual amount of talk, pleasantries, a smidgen of gossip, and the stories Hadassah had heard from her Uncle. It was a rare day when her friends didn't ask her to tell one.

As the sun was getting lower and, for Hadassah, it was time to go home. She had many things to do for Mordecai, the evening meal not being the least of them. She picked up her basket and fabrics and turned to leave after wishing her friends a good evening.

Before she went into her house, she made a stop to check her rose garden. Things were blooming beautifully, but there was one thing that startled her: a worm. Or at least she thought it was a worm. She got down on her knees in front of her roses for a closer look. It wiggled, it was fat and round, but it had dark stripes and what looked like a hundred little feet. She had never seen such a creature before. As she watched, it wiggled past the roses toward the milkweed plants behind. Hadassah decided to ask Mordecai about the wiggler.

He was already home when she got there.

"Uncle Mordecai, do you know what I saw in my ro—?'"

Mordecai was holding up his hand to say something.

"My Little One, I have something to say of the most importance, and I want you to listen to me carefully."

She had never heard him talk in that tone of voice before. She leaned in so she could listen closely.

"From now on, you need to call yourself Esther."

"But—"

"The only 'why' answer you need is that I ask you to be Esther from now on and to never, ever tell anyone you are a Jew."

"All right, Uncle Mordecai, but I don't understand."

"Just know that it's important, Esther. Please grace me with your promise."

"Of course, but I...."

"But now," he interrupted, "I think you were about ready to ask about your roses."

Still stunned by Mordecai's odd request, she had to think for a moment. Remembering, Esther then took Mordecai by the hand and said. "In the rose garden, I saw something that's about as ugly as a worm, or not a worm, could be. It's kind of a greeny color with stripes and dots. And, if you look closely, it seems to have a hundred feet. And it wiggles."

When they reached the garden, there was no sign of it.

"I guess it wiggled away," Mordecai sighed.

"No, no look! It's on the milkweed plant. Just look at the way it eats!"

The wiggler was eating it by cutting through the milkweed leaves in a half circle pattern, making larger half circles with every pass.

"I'm glad it doesn't eat roses!" Esther declared.

"Ah, now I know what it is," Mordecai said, slightly nodding his head. "That repulsive wiggler will someday be a beautiful butterfly."

"That ugly thing? By eating milkweed? How is that possible?"

I'm not privy to such secrets. Let's keep an eye on it together and see what happens. Now, what do we have to eat tonight? I'm as hungry as a lion!"

The next morning, when Esther got to the King's Gate, she could sense strongly that something was very wrong. The streets, usually noisy with vendor's cries and people doing business, were quiet but with a whispering undertone that made her uncomfortable. Naomi was the only person missing from their group, and Naomi was never late. Esther sat down next to Mara and heard an unusual sound. Mara was crying and she had been for some time seeing the tear tracts on her cheeks.

Esther put her sewing basket down. "Okay, ladies, what in the name of all that's full of spice is going on? No Naomi, Mara crying, silence from the rest of you and people in the streets afraid of saying 'boo.'" Her voice rose as she talked and soon she had several people staring at her.

"You mean you don't know?"

"It's all over Susa."

"She's gone, she's gone."

"He threw her out."

"Ho-ho-hold it!" A confused Esther said. "Who is gone, who threw who out, what does Susa know, and no, I don't know. Will someone please tell me?"

Miriam spoke up. "King Xerxes banished Queen Vashti from the kingdom. She left last night."

"Why would he do that?"

"We've heard she betrayed him, but any more details we don't have."

Esther now understood. Betraying the king was one of the worst of the worst. Vashti was lucky the whole town didn't see her hanging from a scaffold this morning. Esther didn't think too much about royalty, but it was very important to Mara who loved the gossip. The others respected the monarchy, and it appeared that this disruption was a grave upset.

Working in such an atmosphere was not something that Esther could stand, so she announced her intentions to go back home, picked up her basket, and told everyone she would be back in the morning. She strode away, back to her pomegranate trees and rose bushes. She had planned to tell her friends about her name change, but it wasn't going to happen that morning.

Two days after banishing Vashti, a proclamation was made up calling for maidens was on the streets. And the gossip began all over again in earnest.

Girls began coming to Susa from many locals, and some from the most remote places in the kingdom all wishing to be the queen. Esther's friends watched the parade come through the King's Gate.

"I wish Hadassah was here" Mara whined. "I'd like to know what she would think of all this hubbub."

"I think it's shameful that these girls want to be queen so blatantly," Naomi said.

"Only one can be queen. What do they do with all the others?" Mara queried.

"They throw them in a ditch, cover them up and everyone forgets about them," Merab answered.

"Oh, don't be a jerk, Merab." Naomi countered.

"Has anyone seen or heard from Hadassah? She seems to have just stopped coming." Miriam asked.

"She went and joined the girls wanting to be queen," said Mara, her voice dripping with sarcasm.

It didn't take long for them to realize that there's a fine line between sarcasm and reality.

Chapter 3

Esther decided not to go to the King's Gate that day either. Although she still needed to tell her friends her new identity, she didn't think she could stand Mara's gossip or the stream of wannabe queens coming through the gate. She sat down by the fire with her sweet kitty by her side and her sewing basket in her lap intending to put in a full day at home when Mordecai came in and wanted to talk.

"Come, Little One, go with me out to your rose garden."

"What's up, Uncle?"

"I think I detected a change in your wiggler, and I wanted you to see it. Remember we were going to watch it together?"

"I do remember!" she said as she sprung up and took his arm. As they walked, she almost stepped on a chameleon that crossed their path. Esther liked the chameleons, not just because they ate the bugs, but they had such sweet faces and they walked funny.

Esther had almost forgotten about the wiggler. And it would be nice to spend some time with Uncle Mordecai. She went to the place where the wiggler was most often seen, the milkweed plant, or what was left of it. There was no worm anywhere. The only abnormal thing she could see was a brownish pod hanging from the milkweed plant.

"There's your wiggler," her uncle pointed out.

"Where?" asked Esther, mystified.

"Right there, in that brown pod."

"I don't understand."

"Remember I told you that the worm would become a butterfly one day? Well, that's what it's doing. It's hiding away while it changes, and in a while it will emerge beautiful, and fly away."

"Where will it go?" Esther asked, quite disappointed.

"No one knows, but it will be back and lay its eggs. Then there will be a mess of little wigglers."

"We better get more milkweed plants!"

Mordecai laughed. "And, Little One, this is where you come in."

"You want me to get the plants?"

Smiling his warmest smile, Mordecai said something Esther wasn't sure she heard correctly. It sounded like, "It's time for you to go to a place where you can change."

She stared at him, and then the tears came. "Uncle Mordecai, don't you want me around anymore? Have I done something wrong?"

"I may call you 'Little One' as I did when you were a baby, but you are almost 17 now, and it's past time for you to start thinking about things other than me. You've never had a young man come calling, although I don't know why. You are a beautiful woman in face and form."

"I am?" She said sniffling back the last of the tears and taking a quick glance down her torso. "But where will I go and make these changes? And what will you do without me?"

"Bless you, child, I'll be fine. I know a trick or two in the kitchen, and I can hire someone to do anything else. As far as where you'll go, I have just the place for you. The Royal Citadel. You'll be close to me, you'll be pampered, and you'll grow into a more beautiful woman. You just have to remember two things: your name is Esther, and you'll never, never tell anyone you are a Jew. From what I've heard around the palace, difficult times may be coming for the Jews.

"But if I go to the Citadel, I'll be like all those wannabes that go past every day at the King's Gate."

"True," Mordecai agreed, "but with your beauty, upbringing and gift for gab, you will go far. Who knows, maybe someday you will be Queen Esther. But in the meantime, you will have a beautiful place to live and the attention you deserve."

"Can I take my sewing with me?"

Mordecai laughed so hard that he made the sky ring.

The next day, Mordecai escorted Esther as far as the King's Gate so she could say goodbye to her friends. Two of them began to cry, three smiled, and one frowned. And Esther never did get to advise them of her name change.

After the goodbyes, Mordecai said that the rest of the way to the Citadel was hers alone. He could not be seen with her or everyone would easily guess she was Jewish. And besides, any man near the women's quarters would get the death penalty. So, Esther picked up her bag and walked courageously toward her future.

She entered the Citadel and was almost blown over by the noise and the clamor. Someone pointed her to a man behind the table who asked her name and where she was from. After that she was told to go to Hegai for living arrangements. Somehow she found him! He looked at her with a critical eye and said, "Come with me. I have the perfect room for you." Entering the room she wondered, "Perfect for whom? A princess?"

It was a splendid room, and she found out quickly that it was one of the nicest rooms in the Citadel. She was then told by other residents that Hegai picks out favorites, and the others wanted to know what she did to get such luxury. Esther had no idea. And later, Hegai sent 7 maids to wait on her, and she was served the finest food in the residence. She knew she should be overwhelmed by the opulence, but when she thought of the simple meals she used to serve Uncle Mordecai, she was homesick.

She staunched her tears and decided she must get to know her surroundings, learn the daily routine and the other women who lived there. Her maids had told her that it was a competitive atmosphere, and there just were no real friendships. Esther thought of all the stories she knew that she used to tell her friends at the King's Gate and wondered how she could get a small audience. It didn't look like it was too possible.

One of the things Esther had in her apartment was a writing desk. She thought that odd, since most women never learned to write. Thankfully, Uncle Mordecai was firm about education and taught her many things. She was grateful that reading and writing were among them. Then she thought, "Since we can't be seen together as that could end in his death, maybe I can find someone to slip my notes to Uncle Mordecai, and that way we can still 'talk' to each other." She immediately thought of Hegai.

Esther also wondered when she was going to see the king, and she was bummed out to discover it would be at least a year before that happened. What would happen between now and then was a deluge of beauty treatments, none of which appealed to her. There was six months of oil of myrrh baths followed by six months of different cosmetic treatments. Esther could already feel her skin uncomfortably peeling away.

And she wondered how Uncle Mordecai was doing.

Chapter 4

Esther had long ago lost track of the months she had been in the Citadel, but she was thankful she no longer had to take those myrrh baths. Although they smelled heavenly, they were rather slimy and greasy. Then there was a nutsy make-up lady Esther laughingly called the Witch. She gave Esther hair treatments followed by scrubbing it all out. Anti-dry skin procedures were rough on her already lovely skin. There was even a glop that the Witch painted all over her including her palms and soles of her feet then scraped off of her. Esther saw no use for it except to inflict pain, but she got five identical treatments and didn't complain. Finally the Witch slowed down and began to experiment with make-up. At least this wasn't painful.

One novelty of being in the Citadel were the mirrors. The only one she had at home was a shiny bronze plate that was anything but smooth: it made it appear that one of her cheeks was bulging, and her opposite eye had disappeared.

Hegai had been a faithful friend through all of her time at the Citadel. He regularly delivered to and received notes from Uncle Mordecai, and she was very grateful for their relationship. Mordecai's life, by his own admission, was rather dull. He said he watched a new generation of the wigglers and added a few more milkweed plants. And he reported that he regularly walked in the King's Garden hoping Hegai would bring him a note. It was always a good day when there was one. He would waste no time in replying to it before Hegai disappeared again.

So many of the women in her Citadel group had gone to see the king, and Esther had wondered when her time would come. She was told that she could take anything she liked into his domain, but she had no idea what. One of the girls wore a full dancing costume, another took a picnic lunch, and a third took a parrot in a cage. What she was going to do with a bird, Esther didn't know. She talked about it to Hegai, and he said for her wear some attractive clothing and to take only her beautiful smile. So when her turn came, that's what she did.

Esther was escorted to the king's living quarters by four palace guards: two behind her and two in front of her. When they reached the quarters, one of the guards announced who they were.

"Sire, I am Malkijah, captain of your guards. We have the lady with us."

"Fine, Malkijah, bring her in." Esther thought he sounded bored. The captain took her by the arm tightly as if he expected her to bolt, and they entered the king's residence. Esther couldn't believe what she saw. Mosaic floors, draperies made out of the same material she used to embroider, a table trimmed in gold leaf with matching chairs, a series of large embroidered chairs that looked very soft and well-used, and bronze and silver lamps everywhere.

A voice asked, "And how are you this evening?" that brought Esther back to Earth. She finally realized the guard had gone and she was being addressed by the king. She fell to her knees and touched the ground with her forehead as Hegai had instructed. The king bent over and picked up her hand, helping her to her feet.

"My, aren't you a beautiful woman. I'm so glad you could join me tonight."

"How kind of your majesty to say so." This was the first time she had ever seen the king, and he was nothing like she had imagined. Xerxes was actually rather plain looking with a battle scar up his left arm, and the makings of a jelly belly. He also had a small nose, blue eyes, and tons of beautiful, thick hair.

Xerxes took her gently by her arm and guided her to the gold leaf table. "Please, sit down while I ring for tea." He seemed to then stop and think for a moment. "Perhaps you would rather have wine?"

"No, Sire, tea will be just fine."

"Esther, uh, it is 'Esther' isn't it?"

She nodded.

"Everyone knows everything about me, but I don't know a thing about you. Why don't you tell me what your life was like before the Citadel ."

What does one say to a king? Esther thought. Her life suited her, but with someone like Xerxes, it would sound deadly dull. She had nothing to lose so she began to talk. She used what Uncle Mordecai called her "gift of gab" and engaged the king in what she hoped was fun and interesting conversation. The two of them talked and laughed for hours. Because they were intent on their conversations, their tea was stone cold by the time they remembered it was there.

"Look, Your Majesty, the sun is coming up."

"What a wonderful way to spend a night, Esther. You will be a wonderful companion!"

"Companion? I'm sorry, I don't understand."

"Esther, I have had tons of girls come through these doors, and each one had some kind of gimmick to get my attention. One of them even brought a parrot because she taught it how to say my name, and the darn thing pooped on me. You, on the other hand, brought only you. I enjoyed each minute we've spent together and I want no other. It's all settled. You will be Queen Esther.

She was crowned the next day in the throne room. She remembered two things that Uncle Mordecai taught her – one, that her name was Esther, and two, never let anyone know she was a Jew. But she added one more thing to remember – never mention Vashti's name.

Xerxes threw a great banquet for all his nobles and officials and called it Esther's Banquet. Xerxes declared a holiday throughout the provinces and distributed gifts wherever his fancy led him.

Esther was moved to the Queen's quarters, which was just a hair less opulent than Xerxes's. She began picking up odds and ends that probably were Vashti's treasures until one of her maids stopped her.

"Majesty, that is not proper for you to do. That's what we're here for. Once we clear all of the old queen's items, what do you want to do with your quarters?"

"You mean decorate it the way I want to?"

"Of course."

It was a small thing, but it made Esther feel powerful in a modest way. She sat down at Vashti's table with paper and pen and began to sketch a plan for the room. "One of the things I'll get rid of first," she thought, "is this ugly table. I'm not going to let anything run my life but me and my own. No memory of Vashti, no Witch and no palace guards!"

Thinking of Uncle Mordecai, she decided on a writing desk. And remembering her sewing, she wanted a cabinet for her threads and other things that she treasured. How much work she would do on her sewing depended on her royal duties, whatever they may be. Her schedule hadn't been revealed yet. She worked on the list into the late afternoon. At the end, she wrote that she wanted a kitten — and she wanted a rose garden.

Chapter 5

Three weeks later, faithful Hegai brought Esther a message from Mordecai. She could tell from the first that this was trouble.

> *E,*
>
> *There is something you need to do, and I ask you urgently to take care of it now! As usual I was at the King's Gate, enjoying the sun, and I heard two men around the corner of the building who were talking. I recognized them, as Bigthana and Teresh, two of the king's guards. It was horrible talk! They were complaining about King Xerxes, and with every complaint they got angrier and angrier until they started making plans to assassinate the king. You must alert the king so those guards can't carry out their plan. Don't wait, Little One, tell the king today! M.*

Esther was terrified with this news and equally what it meant to her. She responded to Mordecai's message with one of her own.

M,

Of course I will let King Xerxes know about the threat, and I will do it today as there is no other choice. Today he is in the throne room working with his lawyers and ministers. Please understand that if I interrupt his work, he could have me killed. But it is necessary that I go. I have faith in myself that I will succeed. E

Esther called her maids to her bedroom and had them dress her in one of her most enchanting outfits. Yes she was scared, but she was on a mission, and she knew the objective was vital.

She walked down the corridor near the throne room, the same room Xerxes placed the royal crown on her head, the same one she wore now. She walked softly so as to not attract his attention – the noise might disturb his work. She found a chair outside the throne room and sat down quietly. Esther could hardly see him through all the other people Xerxes was working with. She sat possibly an hour as quietly as she could. She never took her eyes off of the king."

Suddenly, his eyes shifted, landed on her, passed on to the person next to him, and then flicked back to her. She smiled at him, and, to her relief, he smiled back. Xerxes picked up his golden scepter and extended it out to her, and she came forward and touched the tip of the scepter. With that, Esther knew they would both be safe!

Tears of relief and purpose of her being there tumbled down her cheeks. Xerxes came over to her and tried to comfort her.

"Esther, can you tell me what purpose you had in coming here at the risk of your life, and why you are sobbing so?"

She couldn't keep her knees from buckling and she started to go down, but Xerxes caught her. "Tell me, my sweet, what's wrong?"

Getting control of herself, she admitted that "A man named Mordecai slipped Hegai a note to give to me. It seems that two of your door guards, Bigthana and Teresh have planned to assassinate you." She got it out and felt so much better.

"I know Mordecai, and I also know the guards. I'll take them into custody immediately. Thank you, sweet girl, for being so brave. It appears you have saved my life."

"I believe it's Mordecai that deserves the credit," Esther corrected.

"I'll be sure that Mordecai is thanked for this important service."

Esther was able to get up but with her knees shaking. Somehow she made it back to her apartment.

The butterfly within her was just drying its wings and was getting ready to fly.

Later that day she got the word that Bigthana and Teresh has been taken away and hanged. As much as they deserved it, Esther felt remorse and actually sorry for them. A note from Mordecai followed:

E,

We were lucky, and you were so amazing to get the King's attention.

I know it was at the risk of your life, but what else could you have done? You are wonderful!

M.

Esther was starting to settle into her apartment. After she submitted Her "wish list" to her chief servant, Jaziz, she was almost shocked to see all sorts of things appear and even things she hadn't even asked for!

One morning she was awakened by a chopping sound coming from the Queen's Garden. Jaziz went out and hollered at the two men making the racket. He came back in and reported they were digging a garden for her on the King's order.

She was unable to think of anything to say until she realized this was for her rose garden. Esther directed Jaziz to tell the workmen to finish their work. That meant that soon she could raise her own wigglers! But, she thought, something was missing, but what it was escaped her.

Esther picked up the little kitten she was given: soft grey and white long hair with a pinched little face. She named it Kezia which means "precious". However, this "precious" kitty had a mind of his own. If he wanted to go outside, he somehow managed to get there. Or if he wanted more food, there it was in his dish. Esther suspected her maids who were all susceptible to Kezia's charms. But of course, she was too.

With an easy voice and a smile on her face but with serious undertones, she spoke to her maids, "We must keep a special eye on Kezia. He seems to be running the show because you all give him everything that he wants, good or bad."

Her maids stood very quiet, looking at her, saying nothing.

"If we let him out just because he wants to, he may never be seen again. And if we feed him at his every 'meow', then he'll get fat."

A very loud bell rang at the back of Esther's head.

"It's the milkweed I forgot! How are the wigglers going to get nice and fat without milkweed?"

Looking very confused, her maids continued to stare at her.

"Oh, ladies, wait until I introduce you all to the wigglers. They'll change your lives.

Chapter 6

Xerxes wandered into Esther's apartment one afternoon looking for a little conversation that had nothing to do with being a king. Esther wasn't at home, but the maid assured him she was in the garden, so he went down to find her. Oh, he found her all right, bending over the dirt, her hands and arms covered in soil and water, and a pile of manure by her side. She wasn't just in the garden, she was part of it!

"Here, take this," she said, handing a bunch of muddy greenery over her shoulder, not looking at who was standing there. "Here, take this, will you?" She urged with a touch of annoyance in her voice. Still no one picked it up.

"I probably would but I wouldn't know what to do with it," Xerxes replied, smiling, anxious to see her reaction. As soon as she saw him, she kneeled in respect to him, totally humiliated.

"Now, Esther, you know we have servants to do that for you. I really don't like to see you all full of mud and gunk."

"I'm sorry your majesty, but the gardener refused to put in the milkweed plants I ordered. He said he would have no part in putting weeds in when he spent a large amount of time pulling them out.

"If it would please you, I'll have him beaten."

"Oh, heavens, no! He just wanted my garden to look its best. Frankly, the milkweed is rather scruffy and nowhere the beauty of the roses, but they're necessary."

Xerxes was puzzled, but he had too much kingly pride to let it show. "Why milkweed? Why not some prettier plant?"

Esther said that milkweed is the plant the wigglers like.

Xerxes was confused, and he didn't know where to go from there except to bend the subject a bit. "We have other gardeners. Why didn't you ask one of those?"

"Because gardening is fun and it makes me feel useful."

Now he was stumped. True, he had no idea what a queen did all day. He just expected she would always be there and be beautiful. And, actually, even with the mud and manure, she still looked charming. He bid Esther to her task and walked slowly back to his section of the Citadel thinking as he went.

But she was right! It hardly seemed possible that anyone, especially someone of her intelligence, spectacular looks, and charm would sit still all day. This thought sent his mind into a brainstorm of a number of problems solved.

For some time Xerxes had been looking for a man of enlightenment and visage that people would automatically trust and respect. He had his choices down to three men. One was very short and had a high-pitched voice, and the other was the unmemorable kind of person that melted into the crowd. Both men had high aptitude, but not the sort anyone gave respect to once they saw them. That left only Haman son of Hammedatha the Agagite.

Now here was a man! He was more than knowledgeable and quick-witted, and a countenance that commanded esteem. He had all the qualities that Xerxes had been hunting for.

The next day Xerxes called a meeting with his royal nobles, Carshina, Shethar, Admatha, Tarshish, Meres, Marsina, and Memucan, and informed them that Haman would become the prime minister of the realm, second only to himself. Xerxes was quite proud of himself. After all, he had put a lot of thought into who could fill the office, and he was sure of his choice, especially when Haman confidently strode into the throne room and knelt to the king.

Xerxes wanted to show off his choice for prime minister, so he ordered all royal officials from the King's Gate to kneel down and pay honor to Haman. Mordecai, however, refused to kneel, and no matter how much the others encouraged him to kneel, he would not budge. Mordecai also declined to give anyone an answer why he wouldn't kneel.

Haman was enraged when he found out it was Mordecai that would not kneel to him. After all, he was Haman, the prime minister of the Persian Empire, and it was his right. But Mordecai still refused. He was even more enraged when he found out that Mordecai was a Jew. Haman was never a big fan of Jews. In fact, he hated them. Now he had the power and the will to have Mordecai killed. He was so angry he wanted to have all Jews killed.

"What are you thinking?" a familiar voice brought him back to his feet.

"Oh, Your Majesty, I was just thinking of all the work to be done."

"Anything special? I'd appreciate hearing your ideas."

"When I get things straight in my mind, I'll be glad to share them with you," Haman said.

"That's what I like about you: always thinking. I assume it has to do with the betterment of the Empire? Or maybe it's just a piece of it to start with?"

"No, Sire, I'm thinking of everyone, from all walks of life. I can assure you it'll be a killer.

Xerxes was surprised and delighted to hear all this. He could see this man was looking out for people.

Xerxes had no idea.

Chapter 7

Esther was homesick, but she knew she didn't dare leave the compound. She didn't want to be recognized by someone who only knew her as Hadassah. She had no clothes for the street, only the gowns she wore in the palace, and a couple of old, torn dresses that she wore when she was working in the garden.

She had just finished washing up and was sitting at the chair by the window, feeling a teeny bit sorry for herself when one of her maids asked if there was anything she needed.

"Yes, my old friends from the King's Gate."

"Well, ma'am, you're the queen. All you have to do is send them a directive that they arrive at the Citadel at such and such a time and place and have a reunion."

"Of course," she thought, "I keep forgetting I'm the queen, and if I want something or something to happen, all I have to do is to say so. I guess I need queen lessons,'" she said laughingly to her maid. "I'm going to write out the invitations today, and we'll have a banquet tomorrow."

"Ma'am, we have someone in the palace who writes our invitations. You don't have to do that."

Esther was frustrated. She spoke in a raised voice and said, "I have to be able to do something around here, and I'm going to write my own donkey-tailed invitations!"

The maid backed off, curtsied, and left the room in a hurry.

She sat down at her writing desk and began to compose the invitations. She had everything set for 7:00 the following night. The only thing that had to be done now was to have one of the palace pages deliver them. Esther told them where the group could be found.

"Oh, wait! What about food?" she thought. She rang for one of her maids.

"Yes, ma'am?" Hana said, bowing.

"How do I get to the kitchen? I want to work on the menu."

"What you need to do, ma'am," is to give me a list of what you want and I'll take it to the kitchen."

Preparing the food was the best part of throwing a party. Now she wouldn't be able to even do that. She felt she was back to square one. That feeling of being useless was creeping in again.

"I don't care, I want to see the kitchen," she almost yelled in her frustration. "Now where is it?"

"That is our job, ma'am. Whatever you want…"

"I don't care about who takes what to the kitchen. I'm going to do it and if you give me any grief about it, so help me I'll pull your hair out."

Her maid could see the tears forming in Esther's eyes. Suddenly Esther collapsed and bawled like a baby in Hana's arms until she realized what she was doing. Esther sat up and wiped her eyes.

"You'll forget about this incident, won't you," Esther said, almost begging.

"Yes, ma'am."

Now, what are we going to do about the food?

"It's simple. We'll both go down to the kitchen together. Once you know the way and can stand it, you can go anytime you please."

Esther thought. I wonder what she meant by, "Once you know the way and you can stand it." Well, there's no time like now to find out.

After going through twisting walkways and down a set of stairs longer than she had ever known, they came to the kitchen. Esther expected wonderful smells to be emanating, but all she smelled was old meat. She was beginning to dread what was behind the kitchen door.

After the initial shock of having the queen in the kitchen, the staff bowed to her as she was looking over the kitchen. She finally found the source of the old meat smell, and she asked about it.

"This is the day we hand out pieces of meat to the poor," one of the chefs informed her. We need to get it out of the kitchen before it spoils and give it to people who know to cook it up immediately to stop the spoiling process."

She felt better that she or Xerxes, or anyone else in the Citadel were not recipients. It was time to get down to business, so she told the chef about the banquet and what would he recommend for it. It didn't take long to figure out, and Esther and her maid left. After climbing those stairs and going through the twisted passages, Esther made up her mind: she would let Hana take a list to the kitchen instead of taking it herself.

But what really had her mind in a twitter was what the chef said about meat for the poor. How much of what was in the Citadel was thrown away simply as excess? Or just because it wasn't perfect? Although Xerxes probably wouldn't know, she could summon the person who would. She would start a benevolence system within the Palace!

She found she had been lost in thought for so long that, if it wasn't for one of her maids tapping her on the shoulder, she may have missed her own party.

"Ma'am," Ard said gently. "It's time to get ready for your banquet."

She had totally forgotten about it.

"You must have been washed in some wonderful thought. I wish you could have seen your face! It looked as if it were shining."

"I've just had the most wonderful idea, Ard. I'll share it with you later as it involves my friends, too."

It wasn't long before she could hear giggling, oohing and muffled talking. She stood in her reception hall, dressed in a glorious green gown and had every hair in place. Just for fun, she was hoping they wouldn't know her.

They didn't.

They bowed as they had been told to do. She greeted them with a "good evening." But she knew her voice had given her away when she heard Naomi say, "Hey, Squirt, howya doin'?" The others then also recognized and surrounded her with hugs and questions.

"Why didn't you let us know you were the queen?"

"What's it like to live in this palace?'

"Is the king nice?"

"Is he handsome?"

"Can you eat anything you want?"

"Come on in my dining room and have some something to eat" As they moved down the hall, Mara was rubbernecking so much she wasn't paying attention to where she was going, and she smashed into a pillar knocking herself down. There was no damage, but when they helped her up she was a bit dizzy.

"Can you see how a simple accident like this might turn into street gossip?" Esther pointed out. "People will talk and say, 'A guest at the Queen's dinner party was thrown to the ground by one of the guards when the queen didn't like the woman's table manners.'"

Mara wagged her still dizzy head and said, "Guess gossip about the queen is no longer possible. At least from me. I know you too well. And I can see how the truth can be stretched. From now on, any fudge nuggets I hear about you will be squashed."

They arrived at the dining area with its white and gold draperies wall to wall, the table set with gold goblets and flatware, delicate china plates and tea cups, and tons of food. Esther was amazed what a visit to the kitchen could yield.

"This is schwarma," Esther pointed out, "it's the king's favorite. This, however, is my favorite," she said pointing at the baklava. Everyone dug in.

"Ladies, before the questions begin, and I have a feeling you have a lot of them, I have something to tell you that you must strictly obey." She dismissed her maids and the two guards. Motioning everyone to lean forward to hear, she spoke in a soft voice. "My name is no longer Hadassah. I'm Esther. And I will be to the end of my days. Can you keep that secret and only call me Esther from now on?"

All nodded. "But why the change, Squirt?" Naomi asked. "I'm sorry, your majesty, I mean Esther.'

"I'm sorry, I can't tell you," Esther replied. "Just be sure you remember I'm Esther. Okay, I'll call the maids back in. The guards can stay outside!" They all laughed.

Then the questions began. But she had to be careful because no matter what Mara had said, temptation for gossip was very strong in her.

The maids stood by and listened.

When the questions slowed down, she had the chance to dip into the idea she had after visiting the kitchen.

"Ladies, you should know that being queen isn't all fun and games. In fact, it can be downright boring."

"Bore me, bore me!" Naomi pleaded with a smile.

Esther smiled back. "Yesterday I was down in the kitchen making arrangement for our meal, and they had this gross side of meat that was starting to smell bad and was covered in flies. They told me they were going to cut it up and give it to the poor before it rotted. That started me thinking. No one deserves rotting meat. I don't care how poor or rich, but what can be done about it." At this point she stood up. "For most people, being poor is something for which they have no control. As citizens of Susa, we need to do something about it.

"But what can we do about it? We're just women." Merab whined.

Esther gave Merab a nasty look.

"From what I have seen of the Citadel, and probably what I haven't, there is an awful lot of excess here that is simply discarded. What I need, and from you ladies also," Esther said including the maids, "is to find out what is in short supply in the city, be it food, wood or even clothing, that can be distributed to those who need it but can't get it for whatever reason. But we must have strict permission from the king about this, and I will speak to him about it. Any questions? Any thoughts? I'd like to hear them."

"What else is there for us to do?" Naomi asked.

"Check around with your neighbors, talk to the poor in the streets, find out what it is they are in need of. You can write me a note and give it to my servant, Hegai –- Orpah, will you go ring for Hegai please."

"This sounds like a secret operation," Mara said, making mysterious gestures with her hands.

"No, it is absolutely not! Once I have the king's permission, I want everyone to know about it. Think about all the clothes, for instance, that can be reused. We'll have to have a certain day that the poor can come and pick up certain items. Well, I'll work that out with the king."

Hegai arrived and got the opportunity to meet all Esther's sewing circle. He smiled broadly when he was told he was going to be the courier and promised to be faithful in that duty.

The next morning, Esther was able to track down Xerxes to get his permission for her benevolence project, and she sat with him over tea for more than an hour just explaining what it would entail and who was already involved. Xerxes' order was clear and cold.

"No."

Chapter 8

"I don't understand. What is your reason…"

"I have a few appointments that need to be taken care of," Xerxes commanded, "but first I need the kitchen to stop giving away rotting meat. And then I want you to sit there because I have someone with whom you need to become acquainted."

After he had talked to his servant and had him deliver the message to the kitchen, he rang a bell, and in came a tall, handsome man. Xerxes could see Esther appeared wary of Haman. It disappointed him. But what the duck water! She was just a woman. What did she know?

During the introductions, Esther could quickly see that Haman was an arrogant windbag, and not unwilling to take over Xerxes power. She also thought that he was empty, without a solid thought or ideas totally his own. Just slightly she turned her back on him to make her silent point. Luckily, Xerxes missed that point.

Esther dismissed herself citing she knew they had business to talk over, and Xerxes was pleased with her demeanor, so much so that he didn't even notice she had not been her charming self.

"There is something, your Majesty, I would like to talk over with you before we have any formal meetings with the rest of the ministers," Haman said."

"Oh," Xerxes acknowledged," what could that be?"

Haman took a deep breath. "Are you aware that there are a particular people living among us, scattered all throughout your kingdom who are different? Their ways are strange, and what laws they do have are not like any of the king's laws, nor do they obey the king's laws. Frankly, it's not in your best interest to tolerate them. I think it would be an intelligent move on your part to issue a decree to destroy them. I would put a million dollars in silver in the royal treasury for the men who carry out this task."

"Do these 'particular people' have a name I would recognize?"

"I think so, sire. They are the Jews."

Xerxes was startled. Although he knew Jews were part of the Susa population, and the Persian Empire in general, he was unaware of any irregularities in their behavior. He watched as Haman took a scroll out of his cloak for him to sign.

"This says that the "business" will take place in Adar? queried Xerxes. "That's almost a year away. Where did you come up with that date?"

The left side of the thin mustache on Haman's lip curled in a half smile. "I cast *pur*, and that's the results."

"All right. Lawbreakers in Persia are punished with death anyway. We can't have a whole race of people who can't keep the king's laws."

The king took the signet ring from his finger and gave it to Haman. "Forget the money. Just do what you want with those people."

When all this was done, Xerxes and Haman sat down to drink.

The following day, the thirteenth of the first month, Xerxes called for all the royal secretaries to write out for each of the provinces in their own languages to the King's satraps, the governors, and nobles what would be done on the thirteenth day of Adar. The edict said that all Jews, young and old, male and female were to be annihilated, killed and destroyed, their goods and property plundered. All citizens were to be made aware of this edict so they could prepare for the day. This was signed by Xerxes and impressed with his signet ring.

The city of Susa was dumbstruck.

Chapter 9

It was past three o'clock in the morning, and Esther had been unable to sleep all night. Her bedroom was stuffy, so she opened a window and immediately felt it. It was a dazed, thunderstruck aura as if someone had punched the city with a giant hand. She wanted to catch at least an hour or two of rest, but sleep was just too elusive for her and the city's mood too restless, so she gave up.

She sat down to write a note to her Uncle Mordecai. She hadn't answered his last one. It had wonderful news in it! Without knowing the family ties, Xerxes had made Mordecai a minister in his royal court. Now they really didn't have to write notes to each other since they could talk just about any time they were in the corridors. However she tried to write a note, but the words weren't there.

Nothing seemed to be working that morning. But that was just the start of it all. Her world, seemingly knocked a little sideways, was about to be flattened.

It was from her maids and servants that she first learned about Mordecai's behavior. They told her he was outside the King's Gate, making wailing noises and wearing "odd clothes." She sent more appropriate clothes out to him, but he refused them. Puzzled, but wary, she sent her servant, Hathach, out to find the truth in what he was doing. Mordecai told him everything.

Reporting back, Hathach told Esther of the horror that was contained in the edict from Haman and Xerxes. When Mordecai read it, he tore his clothes and put on sackcloth and ashes, as did many other Jews in Susa. Mordecai told him everything, including the million dollars in silver Haman would pay.

No wonder the city was trembling.

She sent word for Mordecai to come into the palace, but he refused. No one wearing sackcloth was allowed past the King's Gate and far be it from him not to follow the law!

"Tell Mordecai," Esther instructed Hathach, "to gather all the Jews in Susa and fast and pray for three days and nights, and I will do the same with my maids and servants."

Mordecai then, through Hathach, asked Esther to do something that was truly frightening to her: go speak to Xerxes when he is working in his throne room. She knew it may mean the end of her. Anyone who approached the king in his inner court without being summoned was subject to death. But then Mordecai said something only Esther could understand: "You've eaten your milkweed and spent time in your cocoon. I can see you now trying to come out and dry your wings."

"You may choose to not say a thing and escape the consequences," Mordecai pointed out, "but you may lose everyone else in the meantime. If, though, you are, by chance, in the position to help in such a time as this, who's to say you were not meant to do it?"

Esther gathered all her courage and said, "After we have fasted and prayed these three days and nights, I will go to the king, even though it's against the law, and if I perish, then I perish."

Mordecai followed all of Esther's instructions.

It was likely the panic and shock that rattled the city that was the element that kept Esther awake the past night, so in the middle of the afternoon, she fell asleep exhausted. Esther wasn't prone to dreams, or at least those she could remember, but this one stood out as amazingly vivid.

She was in her garden, the garden she kept at Mordecai's house where she first discovered the wigglers, and a myriad of butterflies were drying their wings. Without warning, in a burst of orange, black and white, all the new butterflies rose up and fluttered all over her, the rest of the garden, and Mordecai's house. One landed on her nose and it made her giggle. She could feel its tiny feet digging into her skin trying to hold on. It was like the smallest of artist brushes tickling her. She looked straight ahead and could see the lovely creature's black eyes confidently staring right back at her. With all the other butterflies flitted around her, she felt strength and tranquility.

When she woke, it was almost dark, but she needed to go to her wiggle garden to see if there were any butterflies. When she got there the milkweed was dead and the butterflies had long deserted their home for unknown destinations. And, if Xerxes didn't hand her the golden scepter to her tomorrow, it could be her last day.

And it was dark. Like her soul.

After getting a full nights rest, Esther woke up to a bright day, not at all as she felt. She was very frightened, unsure about anything, and, strangely, she noticed she walked with a wobble. That simply wouldn't do. She had to project an image of surety, stability and honesty. Most of all, she needed to be regal and charming.

Esther asked one of her maids to go to the kitchen and make arrangements for a banquet for three.

"Are you sure you need it today?

"That's what I said, didn't I? I'm not sure, but I think, as your queen, I can ask, and receive, these things at whatever time I need them.

Esther heard herself and was appalled at her tone of voice. *"Remember, Esther,"* she thought to herself, *"to be charming and benevolent."* She smiled at her maid and gave her a piece of her favorite candy.

She had put herself to sleep the night before by mentally going through her closet. She decided on the light blue gown and the diamond tiara. Next morning, she called for her maids, who had been in and out since dawn, and told them what she needed. The gown came out, the tiara, the earrings, even the undergarments, but no shoes.

"And where could they be?" Esther asked.

"You can always wear the white shoes."

"Or the other blue shoes."

"Or your mauve slippers."

"Has your majesty worn light blue shoes with this gown before?"

"Of course I have!" Esther said, voice and body wobbling. She was starting to panic. Without the matching shoes, she would look like a peasant. She had to look regal, charming, and in control. Not only did she need to look in control, but she must be in control. And if she wanted to be in control, she must act.

"Okay, everybody, we're going to find those shoes. Don't stop until you have looked everywhere, even if another of you just finished looking in a spot. And let's not forget outdoors although I can't imagine why they would be out there.

Esther stood back and watched the other's scurry, looking for the illusive shoes. Closets opened and closed, drawers opened and shut, and it wasn't until someone finally went outside that they were found.

"I have them! They're out here behind the big, red pot," Ard triumphantly called. Everyone skittered outside to look. Esther was appalled. Mud was all over the toes as if it had been dragged, and the heels were ragged. There were odd-looking spots on the sides. Esther took a closer look. The odd spots were cat prints, and the ragged heels appear to have been cat-bit and used to drag the shoes through the mud.

Kezia!

"Ladies, we just have to keep shoes out of her…. Look! Do you see what I see over by the wiggle garden?" Another pair of ruined shoes.

"Why a cat would want to play with shoes, I don't know, Majesty."

"We can't punish Kezia for this now."

"What shoes are you going to wear?"

Esther looked at her maids and sighed. She was the one who made a big deal out of the shoes, and it wasn't. The maids all knew about the horrible edict, and they knew what she was about to do. Fuss about shoes was senseless.

"Let's see if there is anything you can do to clean these poor things up," Esther said, giving the shoes to her maids. "I think all they need is a little TLC."

Slowly, she noticed her wobbles were gone and she felt strength come back to her almost empty resolve. She knew now that she could go to that throne room, be noticed, and go in to touch the golden scepter when he offered it. If he offered it. If he didn't and her death was ordered, she hoped she would be strong enough to face the punishment.

The maids helped her dress. Unlike her scarlet gown, the light blue would not shout at the king, but rather, like his favorite perfume, it would whisper she was there. This simply would result in less stress on the king, and more benevolent feelings toward her.

She hoped.

Chapter 10

Although Esther had walked it a hundred times, the main corridor seemed longer than she remembered. The longer she walked it, the heavier her feet became, and soon her legs felt as if they were stuffed full of lead and the corridor was all uphill. Finally the hall to the throne room was in sight, but when she turned onto it, she couldn't get her feet going any faster's than a turtle's. She tried to cheer herself up with the thought, *"All I need is a turtle shell and I'm good to go."*

Finally the throne room appeared, and around it was the hushed buzzing of diplomats, satraps and governors all waiting for their petitions to be heard by the king.

Esther made no move or sign that she needed Xerxes' attention. She thought it best to let things come naturally and allow him to carry on with his business. But that wasn't the way Xerxes saw it. He proffered the golden scepter, and Esther, greatly relieved, came forward to touch it. He told her later that the color she was wearing mesmerized him, and listening to all those men was of no interest to him any longer. He wanted to hear what she had to say.

"What is it that brings you here, Queen Esther? What is it I can do for you? You can have anything up to half of my kingdom."

Esther gathered her strength and charm, bowed in deference to him, and replied, "If it pleases your majesty, I would like to invite you and

Haman to attend a banquet that I have prepared for you. Will you do me such an honor?"

Xerxes summoned Haman and told him that the two of them were going to be Esther's guests and to get rid of all those that came for royal business. There would be more than enough time for them later.

Haman looked surprised and pleased. Esther thought his look was that of a monkey that had just whacked its head.

Making sure that there was no dishonor, Esther walked side by side with the king, ahead of Haman, hoping to bring his giant ego down just a bit for the huge humiliation to come. She wanted to look over her shoulder to see the current look on that devil-man's face, but she decided ignoring him would be enough for now.

When they got to Esther's banquet hall, the found a beautiful spread waiting for them. And, Esther was happy to see, there were her maids, all grinning from ear to ear. And Esther was happy to say that her legs no longer had that stuffed-with-lead handicap. She wanted to reach out to her maids and bless them for being so concerned, and she longed to tell them the corridors of the palace no longer went uphill.

When the banquet began, both Xerxes and Haman started out by drinking wine, and the king asked Esther, "What is your petition? You know it will be given to you. And your request? You may have anything up to half of my kingdom. Even that would be granted."

Unexpectantly, Esther felt her purpose dissolve and her insides froze. She couldn't think of a thing to answer Xerxes' question. Especially not her purpose for Haman. But she could remember that she was the hostess and to make her guests feel comfortable, and both Haman and the king were staring at her, expecting a reply.

So she searched her mind trying to find her "gift of gab" that had gotten her through other awkward situations. This, however, was hardly "awkward." This was a disaster. As much as she had rehearsed the speech, everything had just drained out of her mind. She began to talk about the diplomats she saw in the throne room, and what were they asking for.

After a few minutes of this kind of talk, Xerxes asked her the question again. And again she was struck silent. Then, just in time she thought of the perfect solution. She said, "If the king regards me with favor and if it pleases the king to grant my petition and fulfill my request, let the king and Haman come tomorrow to the banquet I'll prepare for them. Then I'll answer the king's question." Both the king and Haman looked a bit disappointed, but gladly accepted Esther's invitation to the banquet.

Both men got up to leave. After bowing to the king and queen, Haman left toward the door facing the King's Gate. As usual, there was Mordecai at the King's Gate, and just the sight of him enraged Haman.

Xerxes stayed, saying he only would stay a moment.

"What can be your majesty's wish?" she asked. "I will give you anything in my possession, but you know that."

"What I wish is for you to throw away those ratty shoes. I'm glad that when you were in the throne room they couldn't be seen. Go call the cobbler to your apartment. No more ratty."

"But kitty likes ratty," Esther said with a facetious grin.

Xerxes just stared at her blankly until Esther took pity on him and explained the whole thing.

But Haman went home a happy man! He could hardly wait to tell his wife, Zeresh and his ten sons Parshandatha, Dalphon, Aspatha, Portha, Adalia, Aridatha, Parmashta, Arisai, Aridai, and Vaizatha., that he was asked to participate in Queen Esther's banquet that day and there would be another, tomorrow. He spoke to all his family and friends about his vast wealth, many sons and all the honors the king had bestowed.

"Now I normally wouldn't say this, but since I'm among family and friends, and this is a secret I'm sure you can all keep, there is one person I hate above all others, and that's Mordecai the Jew. He sits in the King's Gate for some reason I can't fathom, the king has been giving him honors that elevate him above other nobles. He is becoming more and more powerful. This is one reason I recommended the slaughter of the Jews along with their flaunting of the king's law's among other."

His friends and family were all in agreement. Mordecai must go since he brings out such deep hatred in Haman. Zeresh spoke for them all when she advised Haman have a gallows seventy-five feet high built so everyone could see. Haman liked the idea and had it built.

* * * * * *

Instead of falling off into a deep sleep, Xerxes slept lightly, having silly, disarming, or terrifying dreams. And in between those dreams, he woke fully, then got sleepy and fell into that dream state. One dream he said was quick and very annoying about deer in the palace running at full speed all over the place. A second dream was about Queen Esther, on her knees in front of him thanking him for letting her feed the hungry people of Susa. He would have to think about that again. But the most frightening dream was a huge cat chewing at his shoes while he was still wearing them!

Again he woke fully, but he didn't get sleepy this time. He leaned over the edge of the bed to make sure his slippers weren't ratty, and then he called for his servant. Looking a little bleary-eyed, the servant reported for duty.

"Good morning, Your Majesty. What a beautiful morning this is.

"Is the sun up?" Xerxes growled.

"No, your Majesty," the servant replied humbly.

"Then how can you know what kind of a day it is?"

"It's just the way I feel this morning. Would Your Majesty like a restorative?"

"Yeeeaaaah. That might be a good idea. And from now on, don't go reporting the weather as you feel, but as it is. Think of the way I feel.

Xerxes rang for one of the other servants, and when he showed up, the king asked for this year's chronicle.

Both came at the same time. He chugged the restorative because the taste was too exotic for his liking, not to mention metallic. Then he unrolled the chronicle on the bed and began to study it.

"Oh, piffelfarf!" He exclaimed in frustration. He rang the bell again. Another servant showed up, and Xerxes practically threw the chronicle at him and the king asked, "Can you read?" The servant nodded. "Good! Then you can read this to me. Darn rolled-up paper won't stay unrolled."

After some mundane entries, the servant read about how a man named Mordecai had exposed the plot to kill the king by Bigthana and Teresh, two of the king's guards.

"Has Mordecai ever received an honor or recognition for this service?" Xerxes asked.

No, Sire.

"You mean nothing had been done for him?" The king questioned again.

"No, your majesty, not a thing.

"I know it's early, but who is in the court now?" the king wanted to know.

"Haman just came in." reported his servants.

"Figures," Xerxes mumbled. "Get him up here," he commanded.

Xerxes was beginning to have his doubts about Haman. He seemed to hover around the king instead of remaining at a respectful distance. He didn't have any ideas of his own, except those he borrowed from others and adopted. He liked his ministers to show honest enthusiasm for their positions, but this coming in early bordered on bootlicking. There was no law he had broken, thus no real way to be rid of him. Also he had the sneaking suspicion that Queen Esther didn't trust him, though he didn't know why. But if things worked out this morning with the situation that just fell into his hands, things with Haman had to change 180° for the good or bad, depending which direction he would take.

Haman arrived in the king's apartment, and before the Prime Minister could say "Good Morning," Xerxes said, "What should be done for the man the king would take pleasure in honoring?"

Thinking that there was no one else the king would take more pleasure in honoring than himself, Haman answered, "If it were I that you were going to honor, it would be fitting for you to bring a royal robe that the king has worn and a horse that the king has ridden, and then have one of his majesty's most noble princes lead the horse. This man should go through Susa streets proclaiming, "This is what is done for the man the king takes pleasure in honoring."

Xerxes considered Haman's method and was impressed by his prime minister, his number one, his right hand man to be so humble as to volunteer to lead the honoree through the streets. He decided it was fitting. This was the Haman with whom he was familiar.

"It is done! Gather the robe and the horse and call Mordecai the Jew who is in the King's Gate, and take him around Susa telling everyone how I take pleasure in honoring heroes."

Haman was flabbergasted.

"Well, come on, man! Shake a leg, knock the props out, go! Don't neglect anything you've recommended. Don't forget, you haven't got all day. Remember we have a banquet to go to. "

Haman came back from his state of shock and sped off to do the will of the king. As he disappeared, he could be heard faraway calling to get the horse ready.

Xerxes called for Mordecai to come to the king's apartment. By this time Xerxes was fully dressed for the day, even a little nicer because of the banquet with the queen later. The door was opened for Mordecai by one of the servants, and he came in, bowed to the king, and sat in a chair the king indicated.

"What is it I can do for you, your majesty?

"I want you to take a pony ride, all over town." There was a long pause while Mordecai tried to digest this. The king continued, "It's not as simple as all that. It's rather an intriguing story." He told Mordecai what had transpired that early morning. When he was done, Mordecai smiled a smile of satisfaction.

"Haman is probably waiting for you in the king's circle. You'd best go meet him." As he left, Xerxes smiled the same satisfied smile that Mordecai had shown. He watched out the window as Haman robed Mordecai and gave him a boost up to his horse. As he walked the horse, Haman began shouting, "This is what is done for the man whom the king takes pleasure in honoring."

After the ride was completed, Mordecai returned to the King's Gate as if nothing out of the ordinary had happened. Haman, on the other hand, went home as fast as he could with his face covered. His wife, Zeresh, and his friends were waiting for him when he arrived, and he told them of the ordeal and humiliation he had endured. Zeresh cautioned that he not take any retribution now as Mordecai was an honored Jew and Haman would surely come to ruin.

Just about that time, two of the king's servants arrived at Haman's house and ushered Haman off to the palace for the banquet Queen Esther had prepared.

Meanwhile, before going to the banquet, Xerxes called to the servant who cared for his wardrobe.

"Would you make sure my light green robe is ready? I have a feeling I'm going to need it. And while you're at it, would you give my shoes a good going over. I wouldn't want any of them looking ratty."

Esther sat in a chair not far from her banquet hall. Her hands were so sweaty that they wouldn't even hold each other. She got up and walked, wearing a sliver and pink dress, her favorite diamond tiara, and newly cobbled pink slippers. She looked around at the rooms and rooms of bountifulness and wondered how much it was all worth. She just wanted a tiny bit to give away to the poor. Maybe if she talked to Xerxes again…

A sudden thump brought her back to earth.

"I'm so sorry, your majesty. I didn't mean to scare you," a servant said, apologizing and bowing.

"Thank you for the noise. I have no time for wool gathering, so I needed that thump to wake me up."

Truthfully, she didn't know if she actually wanted to be aware. What was waiting at the banquet was truly terrifying. Good thing Haman was unaware of the words she had been rehearsing over and over most of the night and early this morning. But aware or not, the time rolled on. Esther knew when she heard Xerxes distinct footfalls that there was no stopping time.

"Aren't you beautiful today!" Xerxes proclaimed. Esther smiled, and pulled up her skirt to show him her non-ratty shoes. He laughed and her smile increased.

There was plenty of wine flowing before Xerxes and Esther arrived. Haman didn't spare a drop trying to erase the memory of having to lead Mordecai around the city wearing a robe that he should have worn, and riding a horse that should have been his, and shouting an honor that he felt he earned, not that Jew.

"Is there going to be any wine left for us, Haman?" Xerxes questioned.

Haman was so startled that he jumped up, spilling most of what was left in his cup.

"Your majesty, please pardon me, but all that shouting to honor Mordecai has left my throat very dry." Only then did he remember to bow to the king and queen.

As Xerxes filled his wine cup, he said, "This is the second banquet, and, Esther, you promised to answer my question. Queen Esther, what is your petition, which will surely be given to you, and what is your request? It will be yours up to half of my kingdom."

Esther could feel herself shaking, but this was not time for another cowardly act. She wanted to open her wings and fly. So she did.

"If I have found favor in your eyes, and if it pleases your majesty, my petition is to grant me my life. My request is to spare my people, for we have been sold into destruction, slaughter and annihilation."

Xerxes jumped up and yelled, "Who is he? Who is this person who would dare to do this terrible thing?"

Without hesitation, Esther answered, "The enemy you seek is right here, that vile, evil Haman."

The king threw his wine cup down and walked away and went to Esther's garden. Haman was terrified as he knew the king had already decided his fate. There was no one else to turn to, so he went to the couch where Esther was sitting, knelt down before her, and bowed so low his face touched her.

Just then, the king reentered the banquet hall and found Haman with his head on Esther's lap.

"And look at him! He'll even molest the queen while she's in the house and I am here!"

Guards suddenly appeared and covered Haman's face. Xerxes' servant, Harbona, said, "Near Haman's house is a gallows seventy-five feet high. Haman had it built so he could hang Mordecai, the same man who spoke up to help the king.

"Then hang Haman on it."

Haman was hanged on his own gallows, and the king's fury subsided.

Chapter 11

Esther opened her eyes to see six other pairs looking back at her. She was in her apartment, but she had only scrambled memories how she got there. Then she realized that she had fainted.

"Oh, your majesty is awake, praise be!" Orpah exclaimed. "How are you feeling? Hana, go get her some water."

Hana galloped off making little joyful leaps every once in a while. She came back with the water, and poured the contents of the cup on Esther's head. There was a huge intake of breath all around, and everyone froze.

"Are you trying to drown me, Hana?" Esther sputtered. "What was the purpose of that?" She shook her head trying to expel the water while getting the last of the cobwebs out.

Hana's eyes were downcast and she was shaking. When she found her tongue again, she stammered, "I saw one of the guards fall over like you did and they threw a bucket of water on him, and he woke up. Majesty, mercy, please! I thought I was helping you." Hana's legs folded under her and she sat on the floor and cried, huge gasping sobs.

Orpah handed Esther a large towel and the others helped her off with her clothes and on with a robe. Esther stood up and two of her maids tried to dry off the couch. Esther walked over to the sobbing, shaking Hana and took her chin in her hands.

"Things aren't as black as they may seem, Hana. What you did, you did out of love, so I am willing to drop it. I will if you will."

Tearfully, Hana looked up and nodded.

"Maybe it's just as well. I've never really liked that couch anyway. What would you say, Hana? Green or blue for a replacement?"

Orpah whispered to Hana, "We are so lucky to serve the queen. The king may have marked you for death for this kind of 'attack'." Hana began to sob again.

"Pardon me, your majesty, but Hagai just dropped off this message for you."

"Thank you, Jemimah." She opened it, completely mystified.

E

Beautiful Butterfly, now we will follow you.

M

Leave it to Uncle Mordecai!

And when Esther thought the day couldn't get even more bent into crazy shapes, Hagai arrived with another note, this time from the king.

"Oh, my goodness, ladies, the king wants me to be in his apartment for dinner in just over an hour. Can we get ready by then?" Six heads nodded. "Okay, then, let's go!"

When the guards arrived to escort her to the king's apartment, she was attired in a red bordered gold outfit and a small gold crown on her head. Before she left, she assured her maids, "I'll be back, walking on my own this time, so hold the water!"

The last time the king and queen had almost eaten a meal together seemed like weeks ago. It was just a few hours, and in those few hours, the world was turning at a speed Esther couldn't fathom. She wanted to know how to hold on to something to give her time to think. Unfortunately, she became cognizant of the fact that thinking was too high priced and she would have to go on what she had learned of life since she had come to the Citadel. She knew the next step in getting the Jews off the hit list where Haman had put them was a very simple one. All she had to say was, "Xerxes, I am a Jew, and Mordecai is my uncle." That's all. It made her sick to her stomach to think about it. After all, it was Uncle Mordecai who insisted that she never reveal that she was a Jew.

As Esther arrived at the king's apartment, the guards announced her, then she dismissed them and went into greet Xerxes. He met her with a hug and a kiss, and she noticed there was not a servant in sight. They sat at his table, and he tried, unsuccessfully, to cuddle up.

"What do you want from me, Esther?" Xerxes said in frustration. "I have given everything you have asked for. What more can I do?"

"We need to talk, your majesty." She answered, reminding him of his station.

"Talk, talk, talk, that's all I do on this job is talk. Okay, what do you want to talk about?"

"I think we need discuss the people who have been condemned by Haman. I am one of those people. I am a Jew."

Xerxes stared at her. She held her breath. Finally he said, "That's wonderful! Now it's my turn to let you on to a little secret."

Esther's eyes brightened. "And what is that?" she whispered.

"You should get along just fine with our new prime minister, Mordecai the Jew.

Esther was stunned and happy. "And my side of that story is that Mordecai is my uncle.

Xerxes began to laugh eventually holding his stomach. "And you, you…"he tried to get out between chortles…"won't believe what I did before you arrived." He finished up his merriment with a snicker and a snort.

"What? What did you do?"

"I asked your Uncle Mordecai to join us. Although I was sorry when I got a look at how beautiful you are today."

"Thank you for that, Your Majesty, but we have some very serious subjects to discuss."

"There are always 'serious subjects' to discuss. I wanted to bring some fun into my world. But you are right. And I have something to discuss. Haman, the enemy of the Jews, is gone, and wife, sons and daughters have fled. So what remains is the estate itself? This, my dear Esther, I give to you.

Esther was dumbfounded. She had never owned any property, and in most cases women were not allowed to own chattels. She was also intimidated and would have no idea how to manage such an estate. But then the answer walked in.

"Your Majesty, I have brought Prime Minister Mordecai at your request," The guard announced.

"Fine, fine," Xerxes said. "Let him in."

Esther shivered with joy and anticipation.

Mordecai bowed to the king, then to Esther.

"Sit, Mr. Prime Minister, sit and enjoy a nice meal." Xerxes must have seen the question on Mordecai's face and yes, the king assured him, he had told Esther of his elevation.

"Here, Mr. Prime Minister, "Have a nice cup of wine to celebrate your new station." But Mordecai held up his hand to block the wine. Esther forgot to tell him he didn't drink any more than she did. Which was nothing.

Xerxes signaled his servant and he brought lovely cups of tea for Mordecai and Esther. The not-hot spicy tea was just the way she liked it, and it settled her soul.

Esther announced to Mordecai, "Xerxes gave me Haman's estate just before you came in, and Uncle, I would appreciate it if you would honor me by managing the property for me."

"If I said no, there would be no telling what you would do to me," Mordecai said with a sneaky smile. "Thank you, I will, and I am the one who is honored."

Esther confessed to Mordecai, "Just before you arrived, I told his majesty that you are my uncle." Again he had the question on his face. "Yes, uncle, he is very pleased with this."

Xerxes added, "And at no one can accuse me of nepotism, as other kings have practiced, since I had no idea you were related." He smiled broadly and held his arms, out palms up. "Everybody wins!"

"If I may, your majesty," Mordecai corrected, "nobody wins if this horrid proclamation of Haman's is left intact."

Although she promised herself to act with bravery and be regal, she began to weep, and felt so weak that she fell to the ground.

"Esther, my queen, what is going on with you?"

She replied, keening, "If your majesty is pleased with me, and you think it's the right thing to do, would you write an order to overturn the dispatches that Haman devised and wrote to destroy the Jews in all the realms of your majesty?" At this point, she was so choked up that her tears were soaking the front of her gown. "How can I bear to see my family slaughtered?" One last gasping cry and a huge sniffle ended her breakdown and Xerxes was ready with an answer.

"My little queen," he said helping her off the floor, "I have been thinking a lot about this. The start and stop of it is, I can't do anything about Haman's proclamation, but I can counteract it. You see, when a document not only has my signature on it but the imprint of my signet ring, it's irrevocable. Nothing will change it. But now I have my signet ring back, we can write a document that will fight that cruel and viperous edict of Haman's. Literally."

With that said, he took off his signet ring and handed it to Mordecai.

Chapter 12

When Esther arrived back at her apartment, she found all six of her maids were lined up, and looking at her with pleasant expressions, each exactly the same…except for Hana, who was holding a cup of water. Esther walked down the line, stopped at Hana's place, grabbed the cup, and drank the water. The girls laughed explosively. When they could stop, Orpah managed to say," we were all sure you would empty the cup over Hana's head."

Obviously not thinking about the water, Esther said listlessly, "Business is what I need to talk about. However, first I need to sit down." She went to her couch and her maids sat on the floor around her.

"Right now, as I am speaking to you, the royal secretaries are hard at work, on this day, the twenty-third day of Sivan, the third month, writing a document to counteract Haman's appalling scheme for the annihilation of the Jews. I'm sure you all remember the three-days of fasting and prayer in which we participated, don't you?

All six nodded.

"Are we going to do that again, majesty?"

"It would be a wonderful thing if we could, but I will be needed elsewhere." A couple of the maids looked relieved.

"Back to the document," Esther directed. "You should know that we have a new prime minister they call Mordecai the Jew, and I am proud to say that he is my uncle, a fact King Xerxes didn't know when he made the choice."

"Does that mean you…."

"Yes, and I'm happy to say I'm a Jew, but that's not a fact that should leave this room. Is that understood? And we're getting off the subject again," Esther pointed out wearily. "I want you to understand this edict and know on the 13th of Adar, the twelfth month, what will happen."

"It must be a tremendous trial, for I have never seen you so emotional. But what does it all mean?" Orpha implored.

"Very simple: When he was prime minister, Haman wrote an edict that called for all Jews in the Persian empire be slaughtered, and, even though King Xerxes can't undo Haman's damage, he is writing a counter-edict. This one allows the Jews to fight back. This will be distributed to the satraps, governors and nobles of His Majesty's 127 provinces stretching from India to Cush and all through Susa, each in the proper language. This new edict is signed and sealed with the king's signet ring. They will be sent by mounted couriers who ride the fastest horses especially bred for the king. For the Jews it is a time of happiness, joy, gladness and honor. Is that clear enough?"

"Yes, ma'am," which all six said almost in unison.

"What can I do to help?" Hana asked, almost begging.

"You can all support me by doing what I ask as quickly as you can. On the 13th of Adar, your very lives may depend of a quick response. Understood"

They all nodded.

"And, of course, you know nothing of me being a Jew."

"No, we don't"

"What queen? What Jew?"

"She's no Jew any more than I am."

"What's a Jew?"

"Thank you. With your responses, I now feel more serene and able to function."

Needing to get away from the deadly concerns, she walked outside and went directly to her wiggle garden. She sat down on the nearby bench and a serenity she desperately needed came over her.

It was her habit of talking out things with people who aren't there. First, though, she checked all over to see that no one was there least she be overheard talking to no one and called a witch. She had a leisurely conversation with Mordecai, a spirited one with Xerxes, and a one-sided talk with the wiggles to come. She missed the wiggles, so she got up to check out and see if there was any life there. The milkweed plants, both the ones she put in occasionally and the one the gardener supplied to fill in the gaps, were growing generously. And there, she thought, she saw movement. No, couldn't be, probably just the wind making her think there's movement. Then she saw it again. This was movement! She looked as closely as she could without going cross-eyed to see the tiniest wiggle she had ever seen. As it sat perched on the tip of her finger, she noted its length was half as long as her fingertip was wide. It was so teeny that she couldn't even distinguish features yet.

The tiny creature was returned to the milkweed. Esther looked closely at the area, and behind a large leaf was an even larger leaf full of eggs, and she knew she had to protect the clutch and the wiggles it would produce. After all, like Mordecai said, I am the butterfly now, and they are my children.

Esther went back inside. Her maids were very anxious and, ever since their meeting, wanted to show her they could be up to her standard.

"Jemimah," Esther said to her quietest maid, "I need to find out what the king is doing now. Can you do that for me?"

"Yes, ma'am!" And she curtsied to Esther and hurried out of the room. She was back in five minutes with the news that he was getting ready for a parade.

"A parade?" she said in amazement. "Well, no matter. Thank you, Jemimah. Do you think you can find out if I can have an audience with him?"

"Yes, ma'am!"

Back again in less time, she was panting from running.

"The king said he would allow you to visit. "

"You're quick, Jemimah, and I appreciate your expeditiousness. "The rest of you," she said to the group, "I need to change before I see the king, so help me pick out something." The result was a dark green gown with broad, light green stripes.

She checked her eyes with Orpah to make sure there were no red lines left over from her earlier rain shower. She tried her best to put on an acceptable face. Esther didn't want to show how she really felt: tired and worried. So she went to the king.

Xerxes greeted Esther warmly, and then showed her the scene from his window. It was amazing! Hundreds of people were in the street, waving, dancing and cheering.

Their cheering momentarily turned to madness, and Esther became somewhat alarmed.

"What is making them shout so all of a sudden?" she asked Xerxes.

"I asked Mordecai to make an appearance, and I gave him a purple and white robe to wear. The people are overjoyed!"

"What is this for? Why are they so happy?" She was confused.

"Because of my edict, now the Jews will have a means of defense which they didn't have before."

"They still could have many of them killed by the ones who hate Jews…"

"…and the ones defending the Jews and the Jews themselves will kill those that hate them."

"So they're banking on a standoff." Esther was still puzzled how that could be a good thing.

"But I can see how the people would like a celebration with that vicious edict of Haman's hanging over their heads."

"That's exactly my thought, Esther. As a matter of fact, I've thought of going out there and join the merriment."

"Do you think you ought to?" Esther asked, astonished. "No guards, no weapons, no bowmen?"

"Oh, I'll take guards, all right."

"Your majesty, I have just thought of something: How about I go out with you? I'm sure the people would like to see both their king and their queen. We'll have guards, after all. The people have never seen me. Have they seen you?"

"Well," he hedged, "I do go out, but no so anyone would notice. I dress as a guard, or some other costume. If it's a royal parade, I sit in the sedan chair and I wear my beard. It's probably not the best idea to be recognized though."

"Then it's best to keep it that way, is it not, your majesty?" Esther challenged.

Xerxes heaved a huge sigh, looked out the window again, and then turned his back on all the merriment.

"You are so right, my little queen. I don't belong to that world. I belong in a world of decisions and other people's problems, and that can get rather grim some days. I just thought...."

"...that you could have a little of what they are having now," Esther commiserated. "Your comments over the last few days have convinced me that you are a great king who is devoted to his people."

The king sighed again. "Just as you are devoted, my sweet. But that brings to mind another subject I wanted to discuss with you."

Esther's ears perked up.

"A while back, you asked me about handing out food to needy people, and, at the time I thought it wasn't a good idea, so I said no. I'm not sure why I said that except I felt threatened."

"Threatened, Sire?" How so?"

"As I said, I'm not sure, but what I am sure of is that you could be harmed out there, and I couldn't stand to have anything happen to you." The king's head, slightly bowed by worry and sadness, suddenly popped up. "But, then I realized you just about lived in the streets of Susa with your sewing circle, with some distance to walk to and from your uncle's house. Did anything ever happen?"

Esther shook her head.

"Then I think it's fair to say that you may deliver leftovers from the kitchen of any kind to the poor of the city. But how are you going to find them?"

"Thanks to my sewing circle, that won't be a problem. I should think that I could take one day a week without giving up my duties in the palace, and visit the houses that the women of the circle have scouted out for me. They and I will drop off these bundles, and, hopefully, this will become a tradition of future queens."

"But you must take guards with when you are on the streets," Xerxes reminded her.

Although Esther could not countermand a direct order from the king, she did the only thing she could think of: she pouted.

The face disturbed the king. He wasn't quite able to fathom what it meant, but he also couldn't ignore it. "My queen isn't happy with something. Will you share that with me?"

"Guards!" she almost shouted, "guards, guards, guards!" I'm sick to death of the guards!"

"They're necessary," Xerxes said authoritatively.

Her voice modified to a gentle weariness, "No, dear majesty, they are not. I know people who are terrified of them for whatever reason. Picture this: I come up to a door where I am delivering probably the first substantial meal the people have had in a week. Instead of handing them the package of food, they take a look at a guard, are terrified, and slams the door and locks it. It deprives the household of needed nourishment and increases their fear."

"Then we'll just send guard looking like anyone else in the streets of Susa. And, instead of four guards, I'll cut it down to two."

They sat and talked for a few more hours, forgetting dinner entirely, but Esther didn't care. She was happy in his company.

Before she went to bed, she gave the royal secretary a job: she wanted invitations to all her sewing circle for the next day: their job for the queen was about to begin. Then she asked Jemima if she would go to the kitchen and ask for fifteen loaves of bread for tomorrow. Then she wanted to have a small end of the loaf taken off which could be torn up and scattered for the birds. This way she could tell Xerxes that those loaves were leftovers.

Chapter 13

It was exactly mid-morning when Esther's sewing circle was announced at the palace. Ahead of their appearance, she could hear all seven of them oohing, giggling, and whispering excitedly punctuated by an occasional sneeze. By the time they got to Esther's apartment, and they were properly announced, two of them were almost jumping up and down in excitement eliciting icy stares from Merab and Naomi.

"Good morning my dear friends," Esther said with a good measure of excitement herself.

They gathered in front of her and bowed deeply, then she spread her arms wide and they all came in for a group hug.

"Ah-choo!" came from somewhere in the hug circle.

Esther looked around for the guilty sneezer, and her eyes landed on the one with the teary red eyes and runny nose.

"Hannah, you just shouldn't have come, if you're sick. Come on, lie down on my couch. I'll get you some tea."

"Oh, your majesty, I couldn't miss coming to visit you. It's been so long since we have seen you, that I…I…."

Esther could see the sneeze coming, backed off and ducked.

"Helah," she called for her maid, "Will you get this poor unfortunate a nice cup of tea? In fact, why don't you bring all of us some tea." In the meantime, Jemimah brought Hannah a comforting, soft cloth to wipe her red nose.

"Isn't anyone else afraid she'll catch Hannah's cold?" Esther inquired of the bunch.

Everyone wagged their heads. "Should we be?" asked Naomi.

Esther was rather dumbfounded. "Our royal physician says that just being around someone who is sick can make you sick, too."

"When my uncle broke his leg I went to see him. I didn't get a broken leg," Mara pointed out.

"You can't catch an accident, you can only catch sicknesses," Esther said. "Best advice is to stay away from sick people. So, Hannah, I'm going to ring for my royal carriage to take you home. Would you like that?" Hannah nodded. "And I'm sure the others would be glad to fill you in on what I have to say."

Esther rang for a guard to get the carriage and to escort her. She left happily – and sneezing.

"I'm sure she'll be much happier at home. I would be," Esther said.

Right after Hannah left, a guard came in and announced the king.

"On your knees, ladies," Esther instructed.

The king walked in and saw a group of ladies he didn't know. He commanded them to get up, and six strange faces and Esther popped up.

Esther was appalled hearing a bit of giggling coming from behind her, and turned to stop it with a look, but Xerxes, who was circling the group seemed to enjoy it. Esther dropped it.

"My queen, I see the ladies from the sewing circle are here. Ladies I know you will help her majesty with her project. I just wanted to meet you." He turned on his heel and left, leaving everyone a bit breathless.

"What was that all about? I mean, it was a pleasure to meet him and know what he looks like, but is that a bit strange, Esther?" Azulah asked.

Esther sighed. "That's the king. All business. Sees what he wants to see, learns what he wants to learn, and he's gone."

"And you get along with him?" Mara wanted to know.

"Very well. There are times when we sit and talk for hours, but that's usually in the evening when he's done being king for a while.

There was some giggling from a few of the group, and Esther asked what was going on.

"We just thought you would like to know that Miriam has a secret," Mara said with half a grin.

Esther looked at Miriam and right away she knew. "What's his name and where did you meet him and when's the wedding?"

His name is Talmar and he's a cobbler, and we hope to be married in a few weeks."

"Have you got everything set for your wedding? Would you like to have it at the palace?"

Everyone thought Miriam was going to faint.

"I'd like to, but, but wouldn't the king be upset?"

"Not if he's invited, and not if the wedding is in the evening. He loves a party. And we can't have our palace workers have a little do-nothing wedding. Would you like to first ask Talmar?" She turned away and asked the guard if she could have a copy of his majesty's calendar.

Miriam said in a shaky voice, "Your majesty, I'm just so surprised and happy I just can't think straight."

"I do need to plan, and here is a copy of his majesty's calendar. Come look at it. I have three dates open. Which one would you like? I know you're overwhelmed. I'll leave the calendar on this table, and just give it a while and let it sink in. I have much more to talk about."

Esther looked at Mara, smiling, and asked, "Spread any good rumors lately, Mara?"

"Oh, she spread a beauty about you, your majesty," said Merab.

"Me? What could I have done to deserve such notoriety?" asked Esther.

"I told you!" Mara declared, "It is not a rumor!"

"Oh," said Esther, "this one I have to hear."

"She said that you were the one who got the king to issue the edict that counteracted that awful Haman's decree to kill all the Jews," Merab proudly informed the queen. "I told her not to spread rumors anymore, although she stopped after our last visit here."

"Mara, I think you finally did it," Esther said with an edge in her voice. "You did. You finally got one right on the money. Congratulations!"

Mara stood up with a look of triumph on her face, and she bowed stiffly to her friends and lastly to Esther.

"You all know what the wigglers mean to me?" Everyone nodded. "As a reward for such staunch support, and when they are a bit older, I will give you four wigglers for your own garden, but you must have milkweed.

It's the only thing they'll eat. And you can watch them become butterflies as you grow stronger also."

Mara looked, teary eyed, and said, "I may not be getting married, but it looks like I'm going to be a mother."

The group laughed, and they felt good.

Merab, with a question for Esther asked, "When you were talking about the wedding, you mentioned she was a 'palace worker.' She, nor any of us, work in or for the king. What does that mean?"

"I'll be glad to tell you about it after our noon repast. I thought since we're celebrating Miriam's wedding and Mara's non-gossip, that I would ask for a bit more than just lunch. Let's go in."

It was one of Esther's getting-to-be-famous banquets.

"This is serious food."

"Look! Baklava!"

"Schwarma! Oh, yummy!"

"And tons of honey to go with the yogurt."

Esther was delighted her friends liked the banquet, and she hoped it put them in a good mood for what she was going to ask of them.

"Ladies, may I interrupt your munching for a few minutes to tell you why you were asked here today? It shouldn't take long, and the need is very great."

"What need?"

"For whom?"

"By whom?"

"Oh, come on. What was it we talked about last? The thing I was going to confirm with the king?"

"I remember," Naomi said thoughtfully. "It was something about giving to the poor of Susa,"

Easter was relieved someone remembered. "Thank you Naomi. Anyone else remember that conversation?" Almost all the heads nodded. "Well, now it starts. I'm going to explain my part, then you will hear your part."

"One of the first things I will do is to pass out fifteen loaves of bread to families who are in need. I know where about seven of those loaves should go, you will fill me in with the other eight. Surely each one of you knows a family or two who could use some bread on an empty table as well as any leftovers from the kitchen. I'm going to leave it to you to supply me with names after that.

Also for my part I will be collecting used—and I mean used, not tattered—clothing. If it needs a little embellishment, I can always embroider something, somewhere on the garment. I will take responsibility for collecting the clothes.

Your part will be to create something useful out of the skills you have from the sewing circle. Azubah, you make beautiful garments. Merab, you're the fastest knitter I've ever known, you can easily make blankets for infants and so many other things. Ard, I will need your talent as a basket weaver so we can have enough baskets to pack and tote food. And for the any of the collected clothing in need of such a thing, Hannah's mending skills will truly be an asset."

"There will be days when you will be the actual distributor of the food. It's just a matter of knocking on a door and offering it. I will also be involved in that part of the project. As for the clothing, there will be one day a week when those that need can come to the King's Gate where we will find something suitable. Mind you, we won't distribute rags. We will be giving away used clothing that someone could proudly wear."

"Anyone who works on the project with me will be a servant of the queen and for that there are many privileges. Your wedding, Naomi, comes first to my mind. Once you're admitted to the palace, you may come and visit me if I'm available after your duty is done. And, on top of it, you will receive a salary. Does that interest anyone?" There was a bobbing of heads and excited whispers.

"I will have a list of you duties written up and distributed within two days. By tomorrow there will be edicts about the used clothes around town so everyone will know."

I've given 2 days a week to this project, and I expect you to give one. Please remember that people do not want others to know that they're too poor to buy bread, but they are anxious to have it known they can afford to give away clothes."

"At the end of each week you will come to the palace and hand me what you have, including the names of the people needing bread. I will be putting up notices about the used clothing. On occasion I will do the actual gathering. The king has given permission for that as long as I take guards with me."

"As queen, I can order you to do this, but as your friend I wouldn't do that. What do you think?"

"It has some holes, but think we can help fill them in," Naomi injected.

"I can have five baby blankets by morning," Merab volunteered.

Miriam said sadly, "I usually make only froo-froos with my crocheting. I don't know how much help I can be."

"We'll find something you can do, Miriam. Okay! Anyone have any questions?"

"Can we see your wiggle garden?" asked Mara. After all, I'm going to be their mother, too."

Time went by fast, and things were humming along with Esther's project. She had names upon names of those in need of food, and even more names of people who wanted to donate used clothing. She suspected that the kitchen was adding food in the bread packages that were not leftovers. She never said anything.

It was a joy for her to be outside in familiar digs and even to walk past her old house. He guards walked ten paces behind her and, as Xerxes had promised, were wearing regular clothing. What delighted Esther the most—no one recognized her! Not as the queen, as Esther, as Mordecai's niece, or as Hadassah.

Yet.

Wearing modest clothes much like she used to that Mara found for her, Esther carried her baskets of breads to each house on her list. Most of the time, she found wonderfully welcoming people who were delighted to get the nourishment. There was one, however, that left Esther a bit breathless. When she knocked, the door opened and an elderly man peeked around to see who was there. Esther said she had a nice surprise for him, and when he saw what it was, he picked up the basket and threw it at her. The guards came running to her aid but she held up her hand to stop them. The man slammed the door. The guards picked up the scattered food and put it back in the basket. That was that!

There would be a lot of raw tempers in the months to come.

Chapter 14

As the time grew shorter and the 13th of Adar loomed closer, Esther could feel a change in the atmosphere of city. She detected a division in the populace, almost but not quite choosing up sides. People were being more secretive by gathering and closing their circles to others. Even non-Jews were included in these circles if they had pledged to help the Jews defend themselves. She had to say, though, that Susa was looking stronger! It wasn't unusual to see walls of all types go up in front and even around houses, walls which were made of anything from sand bags to rocks. The people of Susa were determined to protect their own.

Esther wasn't really concerned about herself. Her life was not as important to her as the fate of the Jewish people was. She was terrified that her people would be enslaved, or worse, be wiped out and go extinct. But, then again, she would look around Susa and see the determination her people were showing and felt a renewed sense of unity with them.

She may live in a fortress, but it was not impenetrable, so she collected weapons and instructed her maids how to use them should the occasion unfortunately arise. After all the battles that Xerxes had won, Esther was not worried about him at all, and she loved him too much to even think about being widowed.

However, she did worry about Mordecai. He was an old man and quite a target for those that would have the Jews killed. She was fortunate that he was smart enough, though, to accept her invitation to take refuge in the Citadel with her, her maids, other women and children of the palace, and their guards.

Selfishly and secretly, Esther was glad that if this confrontation had to happen, at least it would be the season when her wigglers wouldn't be around.

The atmosphere on the evening of the 12th of Adar was electric. Esther and her maids could almost feel the crackle in the air. Three of them spent the evening in tears, others were just plain shaking. Esther tried to keep her courage visible so her women could be on an even keel, but it was useless. She had to make them feel safe, and the only place she could think of was the kitchen. Bidding them to follow her, they went through the narrow passage and the long stairs to hide in a room where they couldn't be found. No one with a weapon would even think of going that path what with no room to even swing a small sword much less meet an adversary that far away from their main targets even if they knew where the kitchen was. But it was not for Esther. She needed to be up and near her people when they needed her the most.

Naomi refused to stay in the kitchen. She claimed the place was too dirty and greasy to spend time in at all, and besides, she wanted to be with her queen to help her as much as she could. Esther summoned two of her palace guards and had a bed moved into her room for Naomi.

Before dawn on the 13th of Adar, she awoke to the sound of clanging metal, and she knew it was the sound of swords. She carefully peaked out the window and saw one of her palace guards badly wounded. And there was someone coming up the side of the building, to the very door she entered when she first arrived as a queen wannabe. He didn't last long. The palace was well guarded. From time to time she would see someone coming toward the palace, someone who didn't belong there, but there wasn't a chance he would be spared.

Esther thought of Xerxes and wondered how he fared. He had the sense, several months ago, to gather an army, train them, and have them ready for the confrontation. Although he couldn't be involved in the actual fighting, he was able to direct his army from the palace by way of messenger.

It wasn't until about mid-morning that the first of the couriers' horses came to a halt in the palace compound carrying news of other towns around Susa. It said that the troops of fighters who were against the Jews were doing poorly and they seemed to be afraid of the Jews. Already two towns were in Jewish hands. A cheer went up as this was read.

"We can't let this lead us to think of victory. It is only two towns, and we have a job to do here in Susa," Xerxes reminded the group. "Let's keep our cheers to simply smiles at this point. Do not celebrate until not one of the enemy can stand before us."

But nobles of the provinces, satraps and governors helped the Jews because they were afraid of Mordecai who had grown stronger and stronger as his reputation had spread.

Within the Citadel, five hundred men had been killed along with the ten sons of Haman. The Jews killed their enemies at will, but did not take any plunder. The directive that Haman sent out urged those against the Jews to take their property, but the Jews didn't do this.

In the rest of the provinces, it was reported in all the Jews and their allies killed over seventy-five thousand men, but didn't touch any of the dead men's property.

At this news, the king, elated, said to Esther, "What is it that would seem right to you, my queen? Whatever it is, you know that I will give it to you."

"Let the Jews come together tomorrow and finish what was started here. Let also the bodies of Haman's sons be impaled to add to their disgrace."

It did please the king and it was done. On the 14th of Adar, three hundred more men were killed, but nothing was taken from them.

Esther urged Naomi to retrieve the other maids from the kitchen where they had been an enormous help to keep their people fed. The immediate danger was over and Esther needed their aid in helping the wounded.

As the day went on, more and more good news for the Jews came in by messenger. With almost every message that was read cheers went up, but there was still work to do. The fighting continued, and eventually, in Susa and many rural villages, the fighting continued for another day. There were three hundred more enemies slain in Susa alone. Finally, the Jews rested as their enemies had been slain or dispatched.

On the fifteenth of Adar, there was joy and celebration in Susa. King Xerxes and Queen Esther declared a day of gratification and feasting as the day had been turned from a day of grief to one of gaiety. This was a time to celebrate freedom from conflict and danger. To that effect, Mordecai wrote to all the provinces in Persia that the thirteenth and fourteenth of Adar would be a day of celebration forevermore, and the Jews accepted gladly. When the king had discovered the evil scheme, Xerxes made sure it would come back to haunt Haman by destroying the former prime minister and humiliating his memory for all time. Therefore, Purim has been observed by Jews, family by family, generation to generation in all towns and provinces, states and countries to this very day.

Chapter 15

Summer came to Susa. It was one of the loveliest that Esther could remember, and one of the most tranquil. There was no more talk of the violence that had scorched Susa and the entire empire back in the month of Adar. The Jews had saved themselves and were now the most respected group in Persia, her Uncle Mordecai was prime minister, and she was queen.

She moved among her gardens outside her apartment, but she always came back to her rose garden with a corner of growing milk weed plant. Her wigglers were full grown adults now and they kept her eyes dancing trying to follow their flutterings.

"Pardon me, your majesty," said her maid, "but you have your sewing circle here to see you. Would that be convenient?"

"Oh, my, yes. I'm always anxious to see them."

The sewing circle was now down to four. Hannah, Miriam, Mara and Naomi were the only ones left after the war on the Jews had taken its toll. On the happy side, Miriam was expecting a child any time and was having trouble moving around. She and her husband had been married at the palace about a year ago in a simple, yet elegant service attended by both of their families in addition to the king and queen.

"Your majesty, if it wouldn't cause you any inconvenience, I'd like to take a couple of your palace guards home with me so they can help me just stand up!" Miriam said. "If this child doesn't come soon, I'm going to be in a permanent sitting-down position." They all laughed, but Esther could see from her eyes that she really wasn't kidding.

"You're welcome to borrow Nimrath," Esther said with genuine generosity. "I'm sure he's tired of just standing outside my door.

"My goodness, "observed Mara, "what would Talmar say?"

"Don't tell me you're still dishing the dirt, Mara!" Esther said. "I thought you swore off."

"Beg your pardon, your majesty, but you are mistaken. I no longer pass that sort of garbage on to others. I simply discuss it from its origins and correct the rumor.

"I knew you would be able to take a ball of dirty old yarn and make a beautiful shawl out of it."

"What is it that you needed to see us, your majesty?" Naomi questioned.

"Now that the hullabaloo of the war has settled, we can resume our regular schedule of feeding the poor. Don't worry, Miriam, you'll be excluded until you have weened the child."

"Thank you, your majesty."

"Something wonderful was started at the Purim festival" Esther continued. "I'm sure you all noticed gifts of food being exchanged with friends and the poor were given alms. We must continue the practice with the poor, either in alms or food. And, since we are missing a few of our friends now, we need to recruit more helpers on a volunteer basis. You four, or should I say 'almost five,'" giving Miriam a nod, "are the core group and will continue to meet with me and be given a salary. Does that meet with your approval?"

They all nodded yes except Miriam who was holding her stomach. "Not to worry, "she assured everyone. "It's just the baby being too active.

Ooh! There he goes again.

"Are you sure it's the baby just tossing?" Hannah asked. "Let me remind you, I have had three babies and they all 'tossed' like that when labor started."

"Ah! Oh, that was a good one!" Miriam exclaimed. "Will one of you help me stand up? I feel like I need to walk."

"It's labor all right," Hannah said. "Maybe we should send for her husband."

Esther agreed and called in her guard. "Go to the leather-makers district in the city and find a cobbler named Talmar. Tell him to get to the palace as fast as he can.

Suddenly, Miriam shrieked. "My water just broke! Oh, your majesty, please forgive me."

"Next time you decide to go into labor, stay home," Esther remarked, but with a smile. "Let's have her brought to my inner chamber. It's the most insulated from the rest of the palace so her screams won't be heard as much."

The royal physician was called, and he came in and looked at Miriam.

"Looks like she's in labor, all right," he observed.

Esther thought, "*Thank you so much, Dr. Obvious.*"

"That means you can take care of her. There's nothing to bringing babies into the world. They come out, you cut the cord, and there's a newborn. Easy-peasy!" And he turned around and left.

Esther was stunned.

"Do any of you know what to do for Miriam?"

All heads shook.

"We need a midwife," Hannah said. I had one with each one of my babies, and she was wonderful. I can even give you her name."

"Then do it right away, and we'll send a messenger to find her," Esther said anxiously.

Meanwhile, Miriam continued to scream. Esther was beside herself with worry. She knew having babies was painful and often fatal to both mother and child, but she had never been this close to anyone having them. And Miriam was a dear friend.

Talmar arrived and knelt by his wife. Just then the midwife arrived, also, barely acknowledging the queen. She barked at everyone including Esther to get out of the room and let her work.

A short two and a half hours later, everyone heard a new cry. The midwife came out wiping her hands on her skirt. "She had a hard time, and she isn't in the best of shape right now. But thanks to one of the shortest labors for a first child that I have ever known, I think she'll be all right."

"Is it a boy or a girl?" Talmar asked meekly.

"You have a girl," the midwife said with a smile. "And a healthy one she is, too. She's screaming her head off wanting to be held." The screaming stopped. The midwife looked into the room. "Ah, everything is just fine. Her mom is cuddling her. And yes, Daddy, you can go in now." Talmar quickly complied.

"Now, Mara, I know it's tempting, but I can only hope that you won't start telling everyone that a baby was born in the palace. It could so easily morph into my giving birth, and I died, and the child is weak and they're looking for a new queen. Can you imagine the confusion and ruckus that would cause? I know now that people believe in me, especially since the war on the Jews last Adar. I can't shake that confidence. I am their queen and intend to stay so."

The day's excitement had put too much on Esther, so she left the group promising to take good care of Miriam. They would conclude their meeting at a later time.

She went to where she always did when she was in need of a bit of tranquility. The butterflies were all over her other flowers, stoking up on their sweet nectars for the flight to other realms. As usual, she would be sorry to see them go, but especially this year. Last year, as they were expecting the conflict, she needed her garden more than ever, and the butterflies were there in their time to comfort her.

Esther held out her hand holding a pink daisy, and a butterfly took advantage of the offering and stopped to investigate. Esther could see the creature's tongue darting in and out on various parts of the center of the flower. It felt like a very intimate moment. Then the sweet critter stopped moving, and she could feel its six little feet grabbing her skin with their tiny, invisible spurs just before it took off. She watched it as long as she could until it was indistinguishable from all the others flitting about.

Miriam's little girl would surely be given some wigglers when spring came so she could grow up watching this miracle.

"Ah, my child, here you are," she heard. Mordecai was looking a lot older since the war, but his wise ways always captured her heart. "Are you watching your summer friends? They are beautiful, are they not?"

"Yes, and you're right, Uncle, they are my friends. They settle my spirit and I can see so many generations going all over the world bringing the same tranquility to others.

Esther was surprised and delighted to see Xerxes coming to join them. Usually he was too busy with matters of state to bother with such things, but since Mordecai decided to take a break, he followed his prime minister.

"Those people and their problems can wait today" Xerxes explained. "This is a day to breathe into my soul and settle my off temper and smooth out the ill wills. I should do this more often, Esther. I can see how it affects you, and I really want a bit of that for myself."

"Little one," Mordecai said, "I can't remember the name of the butterfly you love so much. What is it called?

"It's called the Traveler."

"I don't like that. It doesn't fit the creature."

"Well, what would you call it, Uncle?"

"Think where we are. We are in the king's garden, at the king's palace, and the king right here beside us."

"And…."

"I suggest we call it a Monarch."

"And I will make it a law," Xerxes agreed.

And so it was.

man would have been shown such leniency, and pointed to the case of Scott Peterson (who received the death penalty for the murder of his pregnant wife) to indicate that no, a man would not. He also argued that the idea of abuse had been widened to include simple criticism, and should therefore not necessarily be used as defence of murder.

Conversely, there have been many women put in prison for murdering their abusive husbands, some for much longer than Mary Winkler. The 'battered woman defense', or the preferred terminology today of 'battering and its effects', is not a genuine legal defence in itself; it can, however, be used to convince a court of diminished responsibility. Its effectiveness is due to the sympathy that it elicits from jurors, who can be convinced that abuse is a form of provocation, and the murder a form of self defense. Under this defense, Mary's short sentence makes sense.

The case has remained a touch stone with regards to spousal abuse in the U.S. A made-for-TV movie, 'The Pastor's Wife', was released in 2011. It was based on the book of the same title, written by Dianne Fanning, an award winning crime writer. The story was changed somewhat, with the inclusion of a financial subplot involving tax fraud. However, it also made use of real life interviews with people who knew the Winklers- including Matthew's parents. His mother revealed that she could never believe Mary's story. Charles admitted that Mary's story could be true, and that he could forgive her if she confessed her purposeful intention to murder Matthew.

As for the community in which the family had lived, the reaction was largely one of forgiveness. According to members of that community, the town's 'Christian roots and ... its tendency to give people the benefit of the doubt' meant that they took Mary at her word. Mary's quite life in McMinnville and Smithville similarly shows that the American public would rather leave her and her family alone after their painful ordeal.